Sword Against the Sea

An Adaptation of William Butler Yeats' Cuchulain Plays and Poems

by Arthur Feinsod

A SAMUEL FRENCH ACTING EDITION

SAMUEL FRENCH

FOUNDED 1830

SAMUELFRENCH.COM

Samuel French, Inc.   Samuel French Ltd.
45 West 25th Street   52 Fitzroy Street
New York, NY 10010   London W1T 5JR England

www.SamuelFrench.com   www.SamuelFrench-London.co.uk

FOR PRODUCTION INQUIRIES
Info@SamuelFrench.com
1-866-598-8449

MUSIC USE NOTE

IMPORTANT BILLING AND CREDIT REQUIREMENTS

SWORD AGAINST THE SEA was first developed under the title *STA-TIONS OF CUCHULAIN* at Trinity College, Hartford in April, 1999 under the direction of Arthur Feinsod. Original music composed by Gerald Moshell who was also the Music Director. Sets and costumes designed by Crystal Tiala. Lights by Blu. Masks designed by David Watson. The dances were choreographed by BJ Goodwin. The Dramaturg was Laura Blackwell. The cast was as follows:

MALE SINGER	Timothy O'Brien
FEMALE SINGER	Dana Reynolds Rock
CUCHULAIN/SPIRIT OF CUCHULAIN	Matthew Glassman
OLD MAN/BRICRUI	Justin Ball
GUARDIAN OF THE WELL (HAWK WOMAN)/	
WOMAN #1/FAND/MORRIGU	Jacquelyn Maher
AOIFE/WOMAN #3	Cristina Lundy
NEUTRAL PERFORMERS/DANCERS	Michael Burke,
	Laura Blackwell, Justin Ball,
	Javier Chacin, Cristina Lundy
EMER	Paige McGinley
FOOL	Javier Chacin
BLIND MAN	Philip Burgers
YOUNG MAN	Michael Burke
WOMAN #2/EITHNE INGUBA	Megan Shea
SERVANT	Laura Blackwell

SWORD AGAINST THE SEA was first professionally produced in the summer of 2005 at SummerStage (now the Crossroads Repertory Theatre) in Terre Haute, Indiana under the direction of Sam McCready. The set, costumes and masks were designed by Elena Zlotescu. The lighting was designed by R. Michael Ingraham, and Jeff O'Brien designed the sound. The choreographer was Philip Johnston. Christopher Berchild was the dramaturg, Tresa Makosky the stage manager. The production was sponsored by Ned and Phyllis Dye Turner. The cast was as follows:

CUCHULAIN/BRICRIU	Ciarán McCauley
GUARDIAN OF THE WELL/FAND/	
MORRIGU/FIRST WOMAN	Sarah Morris
EMER	Kristin Kundert-Gibbs
EITHNE INGUBA/SECOND WOMAN	Kelsey Hanlon
AOIFE/THIRD WOMAN	Julie Dixon
OLD MAN/BLIND MAN	Mark Douglas Jones
FOOL	Brandon Wentz
CONNLA	Samuel J. Mikeworth
SPIRIT OF CUCHULAIN/CONALL/SERVANT	Peter Papadopoulos
CHORUS	Sam McCready

CHARACTERS

(Conceived for 4 male and 4 female actors, with doubling as suggested below. All characters, except **THE POET,** wear full or half masks.)

THE POET – Doubles as **CONNLA.** He is always present on stage and, when not performing in the **CONNLA** mask, watches from the side, at times adding, moving, removing or adjusting scenery, props or costumes, like the Stage Attendant in the Nō Theater. He may put on his CONNLA mask in full view of the audience and enter the action from where he watches on the side or he may exit, as indicated in the stage directions, and then reenter in the **CONNLA** mask or without it as **THE POET.**

CUCHULAIN (pron. Coo-HULL-en) – Mighty warrior in the ancient province of Ulster.

GUARDIAN OF THE WELL/HAWK WOMAN – A Woman of the Sidhe (pron. SHEE). A shape-changer with other guises: **FIRST WOMAN, FAND** and **MORRIGU** (pron. MAWR-RIH-GOO).

OLD MAN – Doubles as **BLIND MAN** and **BRICRUI.**

AOIFE (pron. EE-fa) – Cuchulain's Mistress. Doubles as **THIRD WOMAN.**

EMER (pron. EE-mer) – Cuchulain's wife.

BLIND MAN

FOOL – Doubles as **SPIRIT OF CUCHULAIN**

FIRST WOMAN, SECOND WOMAN, and **THIRD WOMAN** – Three mysterious peasant women.

CONNLA (pron. COHN-la) – Out-of-wedlock son of Cuchulain and Aoife.

EITHNE INGUBA (pron. EHTH-nah ING-oo-bah) – Doubles as **SECOND WOMAN.**

BRICRIU (pron. BRIH-croo) – Mysterious creature of the sea inhabiting **CUCHULAIN'**s body.

SPIRIT OF CUCHULAIN

PLACE

Various locations in ancient Ireland.

TIME

The action occurs within a forty-year period of ancient times, from Cuchulain's early manhood to his death as an older warrior.

SETTING

Even though the first two productions of *Sword Against the Sea* occurred on non-proscenium stages, the play is here set on a frontal stage, with a full scrim curtain lowered from the flies for the entire play. Behind the scrim should be a 8'-deep area for scenes that have an especially other-worldly cast. For Act One, there needs to be a sunken or slightly raised circular well (2 to 3 feet in diameter) with enough depth so that the source of its glow, later in the action, is not visible to the audience. For the second part of Act One, The Poet covers the well with a unit that includes a glowing fire, spit and fowl. In Act Two, the well and fire are gone, and a simple 7' by 5' bed/platform is placed just downstage of the scrim and should remain there for the rest of the play. For the second part of Act Two, The Poet attaches, to the upstage middle of the bed/platform, a high vertical member that stands for the pillar-stone on which Cuchulain will fasten himself for his death. Properties are few and simple but should be created as if they are part of a sacred ritual. Keeping props and scenic elements spare and symbolic maintains the spirit of the Noh so influential to Yeats. It is recommended that The Poet be placed in the Down Right area, the musicians in the Down Left area, if live music is preferred to recorded music. Music is recommended: 1) to accompany the four Nō-like dances indicated in the text; 2) to aid with transitions between scenes; and 3) for underscoring, especially for the otherworldly scenes, where the music can enhance the hazy faraway atmosphere created by viewing through the scrim. Based on previous productions, keyboard, cello, flute, and percussion go well with the world of this play.

ADAPTOR'S NOTES

Sword Against the Sea is in two acts and follows the chronology of Cuchulain's life as conceived by William Butler Yeats. Act One consists of Yeats' plays *At the Hawk's Well*; a re-contextualized scene from *The Green Helmet*; and a truncated version of *On Baile's Strand*. The first part of Act Two is comprised of a combination of *Fighting the Waves* and *The Only Jealousy of Emer*, the second, *The Death of Cuchulain*. Yeats' "Rose Poems" and other verses about Cuchulain, recited by The Poet, are used as transitions and structural bookends. For a more detailed description of the choices made in adapting *Sword Against the Sea* from William Butler Yeats' Cuchulain works, please see the Postscript. Producers are granted permission to include this explanation (or the full postscript), under Arthur Feinsod's name, in any program or study guide that accompanies a production of this adaptation.

A NOTE TO PRODUCERS

To purchase masks used for the early version of *Sword Against the Sea* (under the title *Stations of Cuchulain*), contact mask designer David Watson at the University of Hartford (dawatson@hartford.edu). To replace The Poet with a male and female singer and to use music composed for *Stations of Cuchulain*, contact Gerald Moshell (Gerald.Moshell@trincoll. edu) for permission and the music as it had been scored for keyboard, cello and flute. Producers may also opt to commission their own music and have selected recited lines sung, especially those here spoken by The Poet (who then may be called The Singer).

AUTHORIZATION

This adaptation of Yeats' Cuchulain plays and poems was approved by Michael and Anne Yeats representing the W.B. Yeats Estate. *Sword Against the Sea* was co-sponsored by the Yeats Society in Sligo, Ireland when it was performed at the Hawk's Well Theatre in 2005 in a performance dedicated to Sam McCready and John Kavanagh.

I have been blessed with having four poets among my closest friends. It is only fitting that I dedicate this adaptation of works by William Butler Yeats to them:

Andrew Davis
Arthur Brown
The late Hugh Ogden
John Kavanagh

*"Think where man's glory most begins and ends
And say my glory was I had such friends."*

- From "The Municipal Gallery Revisited"
By William Butler Yeats

ACT ONE

(AT RISE: In the center of the stage is a well that will later need to glow. There also is a full scrim with about 6 feet of depth behind it. A mysterious cloaked figure, **THE GUARDIAN**, *sits by the well.* **THE POET** *appears from the wings, takes in the scene and then addresses the audience. He remains on stage throughout, watching, perhaps from a stool, and at times moves, adds, removes or adjusts props, scenery or costume pieces as stage attendants have done for centuries as part of Japanese Nō productions.)*

THE POET. I call to the eye of the mind
  A well long choked up and dry
  And boughs long stripped by the wind,
  And I call to the mind's eye
  Pallor of an ivory face,
  Its lofty dissolute air,
  A man climbing up to a place
  The salt sea wind has swept bare.

  The guardian of the well is sitting
  Upon the old grey stone at its side,
  Worn out from raking its dry bed,
  Worn out from gathering up the leaves.
  Her heavy eyes
  Know nothing, or but look upon stone.
  The wind that blows out of the sea
  Turns over the heaped-up leaves at her side;
  They rustle and diminish.

  *(**OLD MAN** enters.)*

THE POET. *(cont.)* That old man climbs up hither,
    Who has been watching by his well
    These fifty years.
    He is doubled up with age;
    The old thorn-trees are doubled so
    Among the rocks where he is climbing.

OLD MAN. *(***OLD MAN** *addresses the* **GUARDIAN***.)*
    Why don't you speak to me? Why don't you say:
    'Are you not weary gathering those sticks?
    Are not your fingers cold?' You have not one word,
    While yesterday you spoke three times. You said:
    'The well is full of hazel leaves.' You said:
    'The wind is from the west.' And after that:
    'If there is rain it's likely there'll be mud.'
    Today you do not speak at all.
    Your eyes are dazed and heavy. If the Sidhe
    Must have a guardian to clean out the well
    And drive the cattle off, they might choose somebody
    That can be pleasant and companionable
    Once in the day. Why do you stare like that?

    *(***CUCHULAIN***, now a young man, enters.)*

    You had that glassy look about the eyes
    Last time it happened. Do you know anything?
    It is enough to drive an old man crazy
    To look all day upon these broken rocks,
    And ragged thorns, and that one stupid face,
    And speak and get no answer.

CUCHULAIN.   Then speak to me,
    For youth is not more patient than old age;
    And though I have trod the rocks for half a day
    I cannot find what I am looking for.

OLD MAN. Who speaks?
Who comes so suddenly into this place
Where nothing thrives? If I may judge by the gold
On head and feet and glittering in your coat,
You are not of those who hate the living world.

CUCHULAIN. I am named Cuchulain, I am Sualtim's son.

OLD MAN. I have never heard that name.

CUCHULAIN. It is not unknown.
I have an ancient house beyond the sea.

OLD MAN. What mischief brings you hither? – you are like those
Who are crazy for the shedding of men's blood,
And for the love of women.

CUCHULAIN. A rumor has led me,
A story told over the wine towards dawn.
I rose from the table, found a boat, spread sail,
And with a lucky wind under the sail
Crossed waves that have seemed charmed, and found this shore.

OLD MAN. There is no house to sack among these hills
Nor beautiful woman to be carried off.

CUCHULAIN. You should be native here, for that rough tongue
Matches the barbarous spot. You can, it may be,
Lead me to what I seek, a well wherein
Three hazels drop their nuts and withered leaves,
And where a solitary girl keeps watch
Among grey boulders. He who drinks, they say,
Of that miraculous water lives forever.

OLD MAN. And are there not before your eyes at the instant
Grey boulders and a solitary girl
And three stripped hazels?

CUCHULAIN. But there is no well.

OLD MAN. Can you see nothing yonder?

CUCHULAIN.   I but see
    A hollow among stones half-full of leaves.

OLD MAN. And do you think so great a gift is found
    By no more toil than spreading out a sail,
    And climbing a steep hill? O, folly of youth,
    Why should that hollow place fill up for you,
    That will not fill for me? I have lain in wait
    For more than fifty years, to find it empty,
    Or but to find the stupid wind of the sea
    Drive round the perishable leaves.

CUCHULAIN.   So it seems
    There is some moment when the water fills it.

OLD MAN. A secret moment that the holy shades
    That dance upon the desolate mountain know,
    And not a living man, and when it comes
    The water has scarce splashed before it is gone.

CUCHULAIN. I will stand here and wait. Why should the
        luck
    Of Sualtim's son desert him now? For never
    Have I had long to wait for anything.

OLD MAN. No! Go from this accursed place! This place
    Belongs to me, that girl there, and those others,
    Deceivers of men.

CUCHULAIN.   And who are you who rail
    Upon those dancers that all others bless?

OLD MAN. One whom the dancers cheat. I came like you
    When young in body and in mind, and blown
    By what had seemed to me a lucky sail.
    The well was dry, I sat upon its edge,
    I waited the miraculous flood, I waited
    While the years passed and withered me away.

OLD MAN. *(cont.)* I have snared the birds for food and eaten grass
    And drunk the rain, and neither in dark nor shine
    Wandered too far away to have heard the splash,
    And yet the dancers have deceived me. Thrice
    I have awakened from a sudden sleep
    To find the stones were wet.

CUCHULAIN.   My luck is strong,
    It will not leave me waiting, nor will they
    That dance among the stones put me asleep;
    If I grow drowsy I can pierce my foot.

OLD MAN. No, do not pierce it, for the foot is tender,
    It feels pain much. But find your sail again
    And leave the well to me, for it belongs
    To all that's old and withered.

CUCHULAIN.   No, I stay.

    (**GUARDIAN OF THE WELL** *gives the cry of the hawk.*)
    There is that bird again.

OLD MAN.   There is no bird.

CUCHULAIN. It sounded like the sudden cry of a hawk,
    But there's no wing in sight. As I came hither
    A great grey hawk swept down out of the sky,
    And though I have hawks in my house, the best
    In the world, I have not seen its like. It flew
    As though it would have torn me with its beak,
    Or blinded me, smiting with that great wing.
    I had to draw my sword to drive it off,
    And after that it flew from rock to rock.
    I pelted it with stones, a good half-hour,
    And just before I had turned the big rock there
    And seen this place, it seemed to vanish away.
    Could I but find a means to bring it down,
    I'd hood it.

OLD MAN.   The Woman of the Sidhe herself,
The mountain witch, the unappeasable shadow.
She is always flitting upon this mountainside,
To allure or to destroy. When she has shown
Herself to the fierce women of the hills
Under that shape they offer sacrifice
And arm for battle. There falls a curse
On all who have gazed in her unmoistened eyes;
So get you gone while you have that proud step
And confident voice, for not a man alive
Has so much luck that he can play with it.
Those that have long to live should fear her most,
The old are cursed already. That curse may be
Never to win a woman's love and keep it;
Or always to mix hatred in the love;
Or it may be that she will kill your children,
That you will find them, their throats torn and bloody,
Or you will be so maddened that you kill them
With your own hand.

CUCHULAIN.   Have you been set down there
To threaten all who come, and scare them off?
You seem as dried up as the leaves and sticks,
As though you had no part in life.

(The **GUARDIAN OF THE WELL** *gives hawk cry again.)*
                    That cry!
There is that cry again. That woman made it,
But why does she cry out as the hawk cries?

OLD MAN. It was her mouth, and yet not she, that cried.
It was that shadow cried behind her mouth;
And now I know why she has been so dumb-struck
All the day through, and had such heavy eyes.

*(***GUARDIAN*** shivers and, with the help of* **THE POET**,
*emerges from the cloak, revealing a costume and mask
that suggest a hawk.)*

OLD MAN. *(cont.)* Look at her shivering now, the terrible life
Is slipping through her veins. She is possessed.
Who knows whom she will murder or betray
Before she awakes in ignorance of it all,
And gathers up the leaves? But they'll be wet;
The water will have come and gone again;
That shivering is the sign. O, get you gone,
At any moment now I shall hear it bubble.
If you are good you will leave it. I am old,
And if I do not drink it now, will never;
I have been watching all my life and maybe
Only a little cupful will bubble up.

CUCHULAIN. I'll take it in my hands. We shall both drink,
And even if there are but a few drops,
Share them.

OLD MAN.   But swear that I may drink the first;
The young are greedy, and if you drink the first
You'll drink it all. Ah, you have looked at her;
She has felt your gaze and turned her eyes on us;
I cannot bear her eyes, they are not of this world,
Nor moist, nor faltering, they are no girl's eyes.

CUCHULAIN. Why do you fix those eyes of a hawk upon me?
I am not afraid of you, bird, woman, or witch.
Do what you will, I shall not leave this place
Till I have grown immortal like yourself.

(**CUCHULAIN** *staggers to his feet and participates in a
Nō-like dance with* **GUARDIAN** *around the well.*)

CUCHULAIN. Run where you will,
Grey bird, you shall be perched upon my wrist.
Some were called queens and yet have been perched
    there.

(The dance continues. The **GUARDIAN OF THE WELL** *mesmerizes and allures* **CUCHULAIN**, *who drops his spear and begins to follow her.* **THE POET** *picks up the spear and looks into the well, then at* **CUCHULAIN**.)*

THE POET. I have heard water splash; it comes; it comes;
Look where it glitters. He has heard the splash;
Look, he has turned his head.

*(***CUCHULAIN** *turns his head but before he can see the water, the* **GUARDIAN** *lures him offstage.)*

He has lost what may not be found
Till men heap his burial-mound
And all the history ends.
He might have lived at his ease,
An old dog's head on his knees,
Among his children and friends.

(The **OLD MAN** *wakes and peers into well.)*

OLD MAN. The accursed shadows have deluded me,
The stones are dark and yet the well is empty;
The water flowed and emptied while I slept.
You have deluded me my whole life through,
Accursed dancers, you have stolen my life.
That there should be such evil in a shadow!

CUCHULAIN. *(re-entering)* She has fled from me and hidden in the rocks.

OLD MAN. She has but led you from the fountain. Look!
Though stones and leaves are dark where it has flowed,
There's not a drop to drink.

*(***OLD MAN** *and* **CUCHULAIN** *look into the empty well, the white light of the well on their faces, as they absorb what has been lost.* **THE POET** *watches them, then turns and addresses the audience.)*

THE POET. Come to me, human faces,
>   Familiar memories;
>   I have found hateful eyes
>   Among the desolate places,
>   Unfaltering, unmoistened eyes.

>   Folly alone I cherish,
>   I choose it for my share;
>   Being but a mouthful of air,
>   I am content to perish;
>   I am but a mouthful of sweet air.

(Sound of battle cries from offstage, accompanied by percussive sounds.)

CUCHULAIN.   What are those cries?
>   What is that sound that runs along the hill?
>   Who are they that beat a sword upon a shield?

OLD MAN. She has roused up the fierce women of the hills,
>   Aoife, and all her troop, to take your life,
>   And never till you are lying in the earth
>   Can you know rest.

CUCHULAIN.   The clash of arms again!

OLD MAN. O, do not go! The mountain is accursed;
>   Stay with me, I have nothing more to lose.
>   I do not now deceive you.

CUCHULAIN.   I will face them.

(CUCHULAIN exits as the light comes up behind the scrim, revealing AOIFE, the warrior queen. CUCHULAIN reenters there, and she draws her sword.)

Aoife, queen of Scotland.

(AOIFE taunts him with the sword and CUCHULAIN responds. CUCHULAIN and AOIFE fight in the form of a highly stylized dance that ends with movements of a sexual nature building to a climax. Blackout behind the scrim, with a cross-fade to light on EMER, in front of the scrim, dyeing fabric at the well as she awaits her beloved.)

THE POET. A man came slowly from the setting sun,
   To Emer, raddling raiment in her dun,
   And said, 'I am that swineherd whom you bid
   Go watch the road between the wood and tide,
   But now I have no need to watch it more.'

*(***CUCHULAIN*** *appears.)*

Then Emer cast the web upon the floor,
And raising arms all raddled with the dye,
Parted her lips with a loud sudden cry.

*(***EMER*** *cries out, drops the fabric and runs into his arms.)*

That swineherd stared upon her face and said,
'No man alive, no man among the dead,
Has won the gold his cars of battle bring.'

(Transition in music and dance to **EMER** *and* **CUCHU-
LAIN***'s wedding.* **THE POET** *picks up fabric and drapes
it over shoulders of* **CUCHULAIN** *and* **EMER** *as if part of
the ritual and then exits.)*

CUCHULAIN. Alive I have been far off in all lands under the
      sun,
   And been no faithful man; but when my story is done
   My fame shall spring up and laugh, and set you high
   above all.

EMER. It is you, not your fame that I love.

CUCHULAIN. You are young, you are wise, you can call
   Some kinder and comelier man that will sit at home in
   the house.

EMER. It is you that I love.

(She recites or sings her vow.)

Nothing that he has done;
His mind that is fire,
His body that is sun,
Have set my head higher

THE POET. *(cont.)* Than all the world's wives.
Himself on the wind
Is the gift that he gives,
Therefore women-kind,
When their eyes have met mine,
Grow cold and grow hot,
Troubled as with wine
By a secret thought,
Preyed upon, fed upon
By jealousy and desire,
For I am moon to that sun,
I am steel to that fire.

(**CUCHULAIN** *rises. Celebratory dance. Behind the scrim,*
AOIFE *appears with her son,* **CONNLA**, *whom she begot*
with **CUCHULAIN**. **AOIFE** *vengefully eyes* **CUCHULAIN**
through the scrim as he dances with **EMER**.*)*

AOIFE.   It is not meet
To idle life away, a common herd. There is a man to
die.

(**AOIFE** *hands* **CONNLA** *her sword.*)

CONNLA. I have long awaited that word.

AOIFE.   You have the heaviest arm under the sky.

CONNLA. Whether under its daylight or its stars,
My father stands amid his battle-cars.

AOIFE. But you have grown to be the taller man.

CONNLA.   My father still stands.

AOIFE. Aged, worn out with wars
On foot, on horseback or in battle-cars.

CONNLA. I only ask what way my journey lies, mother,
For he who made you bitter, made you wise.

AOIFE. The Red Branch knights camp in a great company
Between wood's rim and the horses of the sea.
Go there, but tell your name and lineage to no man.

(CONNLA exits as EMER and CUCHULAIN finish their wedding dance. Lights fade to black. Sound of a tumultuous sea. When the lights come back up, THE POET returns and places a unit consisting of a fire and fowl on a spit above the well. We are on a windswept seashore. BLIND MAN enters carrying a bench. He sits and begins turning the spit. FOOL stands over him, watching hungrily. They are ragged. THREE WOMEN, who are mysterious shadows behind the scrim, are a haunting presence during the following scene. THE POET exits after helping establish the new setting.)

FOOL. What a clever man you are though you are blind! There's nobody with two eyes in his head that is as clever as you are. And what a good cook you are! You take the fowl out of my hands after I have stolen it and plucked it, and you put it on the fire there, and I can go out and run races with the witches at the edge of the waves and get an appetite, and when I've got it, there's the hen waiting inside for me, done to the turn.

BLIND MAN. Done to the turn.

FOOL. I'll be praising you, I'll be praising you while we're eating it, for your good plans and for your good cooking. There's nobody in the world like you, Blind Man. Come, come. Wait a minute. Don't tell it to anybody, Blind Man, but there are some that look for me. There are some that follow me. Boann herself out of the river and Fand out of the deep sea. Witches they are, and they come by in the wind, and they cry, 'Give a kiss, Fool, give a kiss', that's what they cry. The witches can come in, but we won't give them any of the fowl. Let them go back to the sea, let them go back to the sea. I want my dinner.

BLIND MAN. Hush, hush! It is not done yet.

FOOL. You said it was done to a turn.

BLIND MAN. Did I, now? Well, it might be done, and not done. The wings might be white, but the legs might be red. The flesh might stick hard to the bones and not come away in the teeth. But, believe me, Fool, it will be well done before you put your teeth in it.

FOOL. My teeth are growing long with the hunger.

BLIND MAN. I'll tell you a story – I will tell you a story with a fight in it, a story with a champion in it, and a ship and a queen's son that has his mind set on killing somebody that you and I know.

FOOL. Who is that? Who is he coming to kill?

BLIND MAN. Wait, now, till you hear. When you were stealing the fowl, I was lying in a hold in the sand, and I heard men coming with a shuffling sort of noise. They were wounded and groaning.

FOOL. Go on. Tell me about the fight.

BLIND MAN. There had been a fight, a great fight, a tremendous great fight. A young man had landed on the shore, the guardians of the shore had asked his name, and he had refused to tell it, and he had killed one, and others had run away.

FOOL. That's enough. Come on now to the fowl, I wish it was bigger. I wish it was as big as a goose.

BLIND MAN. Hush! I haven't told you all. I know who that young man is. I heard the men who were running away say he had red hair, that he had come from Aoife's country, that he was coming to kill Cuchulain.

FOOL. Nobody can do that.

(He sings.)

Cuchulain has killed kings,

Kings and sons of kings,

Dragons out of the water,

And witches out of the air,

And people out of the woods.

BLIND MAN. Hush! Hush!

FOOL. (still singing)

Witches that steal the milk,

Fomor that steal the children,

Hags that have heads like hares,

FOOL. *(cont.)* Hares that have claws like witches,

All riding a-cock-horse –

(spoken)

Out of the very bottom of the bitter black North.

BLIND MAN. Hush, I say!

FOOL. Does Cuchulain know that he is coming to kill him?

BLIND MAN. How would he know that, with his head in the clouds? He doesn't care for common fighting. Why would he put himself out, and nobody in it but that young man? Now if it were a white fawn that might turn into a queen before morning –

FOOL. Come to the fowl. I wish it was as big as a pig; a fowl with goose grease and pig's crackling.

BLIND MAN. No hurry, no hurry. I know whose son it is. I wouldn't tell anybody else, but I will tell you, – a secret is better to you than your dinner. You like being told secrets.

FOOL. Tell me the secret.

BLIND MAN. That young man is Aoife's son. I am sure it is Aoife's son, it flows in upon me that it is Aoife's son. You have often heard me talking of Aoife, the great woman-fighter Cuchulain mastered in the North?

FOOL. I know, I know. She is one of those fierce queens that live in hungry Scotland.

BLIND MAN. I am sure it is her son. I was in Aoife's country for a long time.

FOOL. That was before you were blinded for putting a curse upon the wind.

BLIND MAN. There was a boy in her house that had her own red color on him, and everybody said he was to be brought up to kill Cuchulain, that she hated Cuchulain. She used to put a helmet on a pillar-stone and call it Cuchulain and set him casting at it.

FOOL. Come to the cooking-pot, my stomach is pinched and rusty. Would you have it to be creaking like a gate?

BLIND MAN. I tell you it's true. And more than that is true. If you listen to what I say, you'll forget your stomach.

FOOL. I won't.

BLIND MAN. Listen. I know who the young man's father is, but I won't say. I would be afraid to say. Ah, Fool, you would forget everything if you could know who the young man's father is.

FOOL. Who is it? Tell me now quick, or I'll shake you. Come, out with it, or I'll shake you.

BLIND MAN. Wait, wait. There's somebody coming... It is Cuchulain who is coming. Go and ask Cuchulain. He'll tell you.

(**CUCHULAIN**, *now a mighty warrior of about forty, enters looking off at people approaching from afar.* **FOOL** *stares in awe at* **CUCHULAIN**, *who ignores* **FOOL**. **BLIND MAN** *takes this opportunity to run off with the fowl.*)

FOOL. I'll ask him. Cuchulain will know. He was in Aoife's country.

(*goes toward* **CUCHULAIN**)

I'll ask him.

(*turns away from him*)

But, no, I won't ask him, I would be afraid.

(*goes toward him*)

Yes, I will ask him. What harm in asking? The Blind Man said I was to ask him.

(*turns away from him*)

No, no. I'll not ask him. He might kill me. I have but killed hens and geese and pigs. He has killed kings.

(*emboldened*)

Who says I'm afraid? I'm not afraid. I'm no coward. I'll ask him.

(*goes to* **CUCHULAIN**, *but then starts shaking all over*)

FOOL. *(cont.)* No, no, Cuchulain, I'm not going to ask you.

(*He sings.*)

He has killed kings,
Kings and the sons of kings,
Dragons out of the water,
And witches out of the air
And people out of the woods.

(**CONNLA**, **CUCHULAIN**'s *son by* **AOIFE**, *enters on the opposite side of the stage from* **CUCHULAIN**. *He and* **CUCHULAIN** *stare across at one another.* **THE WOMEN** *behind the scrim speak in distorted whispered sounds.*)

WOMEN. Those wild hands that have embraced
All this body can but shove
At the burning wheel of love
Till the side of hate comes up.
Therefore in this ancient cup
May the sword-blades drink their fill
Of the home-brew there, until
They will have for masters, none
But the threshold and hearthstone.

(**CONNLA** *draws his sword on* **CUCHULAIN**. *The light behind the scrim fades out.*)

CONNLA. I am of Aoife's country.

CUCHULAIN. Put up your sword. Aoife is far away.

CONNLA. I have come alone into the midst of you
To weigh this sword against Cuchulain's sword.

CUCHULAIN. And are you noble?

CONNLA.   I am under bonds
To tell my name to no man; but it's noble.
I, too, am of that ancient seed, and carry
The signs about this body and in these bones.

CUCHULAIN. And you speak highly, too. You are from the
    North,
    Where there are many that have that tint of hair –
    Red-brown, the light red-brown. Come nearer, boy,
    For I would have another look at you.
    There's more likeness – a pale, a stone-pale cheek.
    What brought you, boy? Have you no fear of death?

CONNLA. Whether I live or die is in the gods' hands.

CUCHULAIN. That is all words, all words; a young man's
    talk.
    Let's see that arm. I'll see it if I choose.
    That arm had a good father and a good mother,
    But it is not like this.

CONNLA.   You are mocking me;
    You think I am not worthy to be fought.
    But I'll not wrangle but with this talkative knife.

CUCHULAIN. Put up your sword; I am not mocking you.
    I'd have you for my friend, but if it's not
    Because you have a hot heart and a cold eye,
    I cannot tell the reason.

CONNLA. There is no man I'd sooner have my friend
    Than you, whose name has gone about the world
    As if it had been the wind; but Aoife'd say
    I had turned coward.

CUCHULAIN.   I will give you gifts
    That Aoife'll know, and all her people know,
    To have come from me.

(As he unfastens cloak, strange otherwordly music plays.
THREE WOMEN *enter, now downstage of the scrim. The*
FIRST WOMAN *stands alone, holding a large bowl. The*
SECOND & THIRD WOMEN *take the coat from him and*
move toward **CONNLA.** *)*

                            My father gave me this.
    He came to try me, rising up at dawn
    Out of the cold dark of the rich sea.

CUCHULAIN. *(cont.)* He challenged me to battle, but before
My sword had touched his sword, told me his name,
Gave me his cloak, and vanished. It was woven
By women of the Country-under-Wave
Out of the fleeces of the sea.
I have no son, no one to pay my debts, no one
To put a stone over me when I die.

(**SECOND & THIRD WOMEN** *spread cloak over* **CONNLA**'s *shoulders.*)

CUCHULAIN. *(cont.)*   Here. Tell Aoife
I was afraid, or tell her what you will.
No; tell her that I heard a raven croak
On the north side of the house, and was afraid.

FIRST WOMAN. Some witch has worked upon your mind, Cuchulain.

THREE WOMEN. Yes, witchcraft!

SECOND WOMAN. Witchcraft!

CUCHULAIN. No witch, no witchcraft.

His head is like a woman's head
I had a fancy for.

SECOND WOMAN. The head of the young man *seemed* like a woman's
You'd had a fancy for.

CUCHULAIN. Nine queens out of the Country-under Wave
Have woven it out of the fleeces of the sea
And they were long embroidering at it.

FIRST WOMAN. No more of this. We will not have this friendship.

THIRD WOMAN. A witch of the air
Can make a leaf confound us with memories.

FIRST WOMAN. They run upon the wind and hurl the spells
That make us nothing, out of the invisible wind.

CUCHULAIN. Yes, witchcraft! Witchcraft! Witches of the air!

(To **CONNLA,** *accusingly, draws sword.)*

Why did you let them? Who was it set you to this work?

CONNLA. But...but I did not.

CUCHULAIN. Out, out! Now it's sword on sword!

Out, I say, out, out!

(They exchange blows and exit fighting. **FIRST WOMAN** *runs downstage and places her large bowl on ground; the other two follow and surround it.* **FIRST WOMAN** *looks into it as she holds it within both hands, her eyes widening. Suddenly she screams.)*

FIRST WOMAN. I have seen, I have seen!

SECOND WOMAN. What do you cry aloud?

FIRST WOMAN. The Ever-living have shown me what's to come.

THIRD WOMAN. How? Where?

FIRST WOMAN. In the ashes of the bowl.

SECOND WOMAN. While you were holding it between your hands?

THIRD WOMAN. Speak quickly!

FIRST WOMAN. I have seen Cuchulain's roof-tree Leap into fire, and the walls split and blacken.

SECOND WOMAN. *(staring off where* **CUCHULAIN** *and* **CONNLA** *exited)* Cuchulain has gone out to die.

THIRD WOMAN. O! O!

SECOND WOMAN. Who could have thought that one so great as he

Should meet his end at this unnoted sword!

FIRST WOMAN. *(They all stare out.)*

Life drifts between a fool and a blind man

To the end, and nobody can know his end.

SECOND WOMAN. Come, look upon the quenching of this greatness.

(**SECOND WOMAN** *leads the other two in the direction where* **CONNLA** *and* **CUCHULAIN** *exited. Enter* **FOOL**, *dragging* **BLIND MAN**.)

FOOL. You have eaten it, you have eaten it! You have left me nothing but the bones.

BLIND MAN. O, that I should have to endure such a plague! O, I ache all over! O, I am pulled to pieces! This is the way you pay me all the good I have done you.

FOOL. You have eaten it! You have told me lies. I might have known you had eaten it when I saw your slow, sleepy walk.

BLIND MAN. What would have happened to you but for me, and you without your wits? If I did not take care of you, what would you do for food and warmth?

FOOL. You take care of me? You stay safe, and send me into every kind of danger. You sent me down the cliff for gulls' eggs while you warmed your blind eyes in the sun; and then you ate all that were good for food. You left me the eggs that were neither egg nor bird.

(**BLIND MAN** *tries to rise;* **FOOL** *sits on him to keep him down*.)

Ah! You would get away, would you? Lie there! Lie there! No, you won't get away! Lie there!

BLIND MAN. O, good Fool! Listen to me. Think of the care I have taken of you. I have brought you to many a warm hearth, where there was a good welcome for you, but you would not stay there; you were always wandering about.

FOOL. The last time you brought me in, it was not I who wandered away, but you that got put out because you took the pig's foot out of the pot when nobody was looking. Keep quiet, now!

CUCHULAIN. *(rushing in, laughing triumphantly)* Witchcraft! There is not witchcraft on the earth, or among the witches of the air, that these hands cannot break.

FOOL. Listen to me, Cuchulain. I left him turning the fowl at the fire. He ate it all, though I had stolen it. He left me nothing but the feathers.

(CUCHULAIN sits on long bench.)

BLIND MAN. I gave him what he likes best. You do not know how vain this Fool is. He likes nothing so well as a feather.

FOOL. *(sits next to CUCHULAIN on bench)* He left me nothing but the bones and feathers. Nothing but the feathers, though I had stolen it.

CUCHULAIN. Quarrels here, too! What is there between you two that is worth a quarrel? Out with it!

BLIND MAN. *(Sits on other side of CUCHULAIN on the bench.)* Where would he be but for me? I must be always thinking – thinking to get food for the two of us, and when we've got it, if the moon is at the full or the tide on the turn, he'll leave the rabbit in the snare till it is full of maggots, or let the trout slip back through his hands into the stream.

FOOL. *(FOOL sings simultaneously with BLIND MAN's speech above, covering ears to block out what BLIND MAN is saying.)* When you were an acorn on the tree-top,

Then was I an eagle-cock;

Now that you are a withered old block,

Still am I an eagle-cock.

BLIND MAN. Listen to him, now. That's the sort of talk I have to put up with day in and day out.

(CUCHULAIN takes a handful of feathers out the FOOL's pouch and wipes the blood from his sword with them.)

FOOL. He has taken my feathers to wipe his sword. It is blood that he is wiping from his sword.

CUCHULAIN. They are standing about his body. They will not awaken him, for all his witchcraft.

BLIND MAN. It is that young champion that he has killed. He that came out of Aoife's country.

CUCHULAIN. He thought to have saved himself with witchcraft.

FOOL. That Blind Man there said he would kill you. He came from Aoife's country to kill you. That Blind Man said they had taught him every kind of weapon that he might do it. But I always knew that you would kill him.

CUCHULAIN. *(to* **BLIND MAN***)* You knew him, then?

BLIND MAN. I saw him, when I had my eyes, in Aoife's country.

CUCHULAIN. You were in Aoife's country?

BLIND MAN. I knew him and his mother there.

CUCHULAIN. He was about to speak of her when he died.

BLIND MAN. He was a queen's son.

CUCHULAIN. What queen? What queen?

> *(seizes* **BLIND MAN***)*

> Was it Scathach? There were many queens. All the rulers there were queens.

BLIND MAN. No, not Scathach.

CUCHULAIN. It was Uathach, then? Speak! Speak!

BLIND MAN. I cannot speak; you are clutching me too tightly.

> *(***CUCHULAIN*** lets him go.)*

> I cannot remember who it was. I am not certain. It was some queen.

FOOL. He said a while ago that the young man was Aoife's son.

CUCHULAIN. She? No, no! She had no son when I was there.

FOOL. That Blind Man there said that she owned him for her son.

CUCHULAIN. I had rather he had been some other woman's son. What father had he? A soldier out of Alba? She was an amorous woman – a proud, pale, amorous woman.

BLIND MAN. None knew whose son he was.

CUCHULAIN. None knew! Did you know, old listener at doors?

BLIND MAN. No, no; I knew nothing.

FOOL. He said a while ago that he heard Aoife boast that she'd never but the one lover, and he the only man that had overcome her in battle.

(**CUCHULAIN** *begins to shake, which shakes the bench and the others.*)

BLIND MAN. Somebody is trembling, Fool! The bench is shaking. Why are you trembling? Is Cuchulain going to hurt us? It was not I who told you, Cuchulain.

FOOL. It is Cuchulain who is trembling. It is Cuchulain who is shaking the bench.

BLIND MAN. It is his own son he has slain.

(*Sound of waves grows as* **WOMEN** *enter with two long pieces of blue silk.* **WOMAN #1** *holds one end of a piece as* **WOMAN #2** *carries the other end to the other side of the stage.* **WOMAN #3** *gives an end to* **THE POET** *and she, too, walks across the stage. The four kneel and, starting slow, agitate the silk until the two pieces become a flapping swirling ocean of crashing waves. Drawing his sword,* **CUCHULAIN** *rises and slowly walks toward the waves.*)

FOOL. They are all about the young man. Cuchulain is standing still. There is a great wave going to break, and he is looking out at it. Ah! Now he is running down to the sea, but he is holding up his sword as if he were going into a fight.

(**CUCHULAIN** *begins a dance of fighting the waves with sword, working up to a waspish frenzy amid the flapping swirling blue silk created by the* **THREE WOMEN** *and* **THE POET.**)

Well struck! Well struck!

BLIND MAN. What is he doing now?

(**THE FOOL** *climbs up on the bench and looks downstage.*)

FOOL. O! he is fighting the waves! There, he has struck at a big one! He has struck the crown off it; he has made the foam fly. There again, another big one!

BLIND MAN. Where are the people? What are the people doing?

FOOL. They are shouting and running down to the shore. They are all running.

BLIND MAN. You say they are running out of the houses? There will be nobody left in the houses. Listen, Fool!

(*The* **BLIND MAN** *begins to sneak toward one side of the stage.* **CUCHULAIN**, *becoming mastered by the waves, keeps struggling to his feet.*)

FOOL. There, he is down. He is up again. He is going out in the deep water. There is a big wave. It has gone over him. I cannot see him now. He has killed kings and giants, but the waves have mastered him, the waves have mastered him!

BLIND MAN. Come here, Fool!

FOOL. The waves have mastered him.

BLIND MAN. Come here!

FOOL. The waves have mastered him.

BLIND MAN. Come here, I say.

FOOL. (*Jumps down off the bench and joins the* **BLIND MAN** *near exit.*) What is it?

BLIND MAN. There will be nobody in the houses. Come this way; come quickly! The ovens will be full. We will put our hands into the ovens.

(**FOOL** *and* **BLIND MAN** *exit.* **CUCHULAIN** *has been overcome by waves, seemingly drowned. The "waves" recede.* **EMER** *enters and runs to* **CUCHULAIN**. *She kneels before him as the* **WOMEN** *drag the blue silk behind them as they walk off stage in opposite directions.* **EMER** *cradles his lifeless body and rocks him.* **THE POET** *watches, then turns to the audience and speaks.*)

THE POET. Red Rose, proud Rose, sad Rose of all my days!
Come near me, while I sing the ancient ways:
Cuchulain battling with the bitter tide;
The Druid, grey, wood-nurtured, quiet-eyed,
Who cast round Fergus dreams, and ruin untold;
And thine own sadness, whereof stars, grown old
In dancing silver-sandalled on the sea,
Sing in their high and lonely melody.
Come near, that no more blinded by man's fate,
I find under the boughs of love and hate,
In all poor foolish things that live a day,
Eternal beauty wandering on her way.

(blackout)

End of Act One

ACT TWO

(Interior of a fisherman's cottage consisting only of a 5' x 7' bed/platform just downstage of the scrim, with stools beside it. There is a smoldering fire downstage. **EMER** *is kneeling by* **CUCHULAIN**, *who is stretched out on the bed/platform and covered by grave clothes.)*

THE POET. I call before your eyes a roof
With cross-beams darkened by smoke;
A fisher's net hangs from a beam,
A long oar lies against the wall.
I call up a poor fisher's house;
A man lies dead or swooning,
That amorous man,
That amorous, violent man, renowned Cuchulain,
Queen Emer at his side.
At her own bidding all the rest have gone;

But now one comes on hesitating feet,
Young Eithne Inguba, Cuchulain's mistress.
She stands a moment in the open door.
Beyond the open door the bitter sea,
The shining, bitter sea is crying out.

White shell, white wing!
I will not choose for my friend
A frail, unserviceable thing
That drifts and dreams, and but knows

That waters are without end
And that wind blows.

EMER. Come here, come sit beside the bed; do not be afraid, it was I that sent for you, Eithne Inguba.

EITHNE INGUBA. No, madam, I have wronged you too deeply to sit there.

EMER. We two alone of all the people in the world have the right to watch together here because we have loved him best.

EITHNE INGUBA. *(She crosses to a stool and sits beside the bed.)* Is he dead?

EMER. The fishermen think him dead; it was they that put the grave clothes upon him.

EITHNE INGUBA. *(feeling the body)* He is cold. There is no breath upon his lips.

EMER. Those who win the terrible friendship of the gods sometimes lie a long time as if dead.

EITHNE INGUBA. I have heard of such things; the very heart stops and yet they live after. What happened?

EMER. He fought and killed an unknown man, and found after that it was his own son.

EITHNE INGUBA. A son of yours and his?

EMER. So that is your first thought! His and mine.

(She laughs.)

Did you think that he belonged to you and me alone? He loved women before he heard our names, and he will love women after he has forgotten us both. The man he killed was the son of some wild woman he loved long ago, and I think he loved her better than he has loved you or me.

EITHNE INGUBA. That is natural; he must have been young in those days.

EMER. When he heard the name of the man he had killed, and the name of that man's mother, he went out of his senses utterly. He ran into the sea, and with sword in hand he fought the deathless sea. Of all the many men who had stood there to look at the fight, not one

dared stop him or even call his name; they stood in a
kind of stupor. Collected together in a bunch like cattle
in a storm, until, fixing his eyes as if upon some new
enemy, he waded out further still and the waves swept
over him.

EITHNE INGUBA. He is dead indeed, and he has been
drowned in the sea.

EMER. He is not dead.

EITHNE INGUBA. He is dead, and you have not kissed his
lips nor laid your head upon his breast.

EMER. That is some changeling they have put there, some
image of somebody or something bewitched in his likeness, a sea-washed log, it may be, or some old spirit. I
would throw it into the fire, but I dare not. They have
Cuchulain for a hostage.

EITHNE INGUBA. I have heard of such changelings.

EMER. Before you came I called his name again and again. I
told him that Queen Maeve and all her Connacht men
are marching north and east, and that there is none
but he to make a stand against them, but he would not
hear me. I am but his wife, and a man grows tired of a
wife. But if you call upon him with that sweet voice, that
voice that is so dear to him, he cannot help but listen.

EITHNE INGUBA. I am but his newest love, and in the end
he will turn to the woman who has loved him longest,
who has kept the house for him, no matter where he
strayed or to whom.

EMER. I have indeed that hope, the hope that some day he
and I will sit together at the fire as when we were first
married.

EITHNE INGUBA. Women like me awake a violent love for a
while, and when the time is over are flung into some
corner like an old eggshell.

(She sits and pulls the stool closer to the bed.)

Cuchulain, listen!

EMER. No, not yet; for first I must cover up his face, I must
hide him from the sea. I must throw new logs upon the

fire and stir the half-burnt logs into a flame. The sea is full of enchantment, whatever lies on that bed is from the sea, but all enchantments dread the hearth-fire.

(EMER tends the fire, creating a new and eerie light.)

Call on Cuchulain now.

EITHNE INGUBA. Can you hear my voice, Cuchulain?

EMER. Bend over whatever thing lies there, call out dear secrets and speak to it as though it were his very self.

EITHNE INGUBA. Cuchulain, listen!

EMER. Those are timid words. To be afraid because his wife is standing by when there is so great need but proves that he chose badly. Remember who you are and who he is, that we are two women struggling with the sea.

EITHNE INGUBA. O my beloved! Pardon me, pardon me that I could be ashamed when you were in such need. Never did I send a message, never did I call your name, scarce had I a longing for your company but that you have known and come. Remember that never up to this hour have you been silent when I would have you speak; remember that I have always made you talkative. If you are not lying there, if that is some stranger or someone or something bewitched into your likeness, drive it away; remember that for someone to take your likeness from you is a great insult. If you are lying there, stretch out your arms and speak; open your mouth and speak.

(She turns to EMER.)

He does not hear me; no sound reaches him; or it reaches him and he cannot speak.

EMER. Then kiss him; these things are a great mystery, and maybe his mouth will feel the pressure of your mouth upon his and may reach him where he is.

EITHNE INGUBA. *(She is about to kiss him but then starts back.)* It is no man. I felt some evil thing that dried my heart when my lips touched it.

EMER. No, his body stirs, the pressure of your mouth has called him. He has thrown the changeling out.

EITHNE INGUBA. *(Draws back further as withered arm appears from beneath grave clothes.)* Look at that hand! That hand is withered to the bone.

EMER. What are you, what do you come for, and from where?

*(**BRICRIU** ascends from just on the scrim side of **CUCHU-LAIN**'s deathbed. His mask is a twisted version of **CUCHULAIN**'s.)*

BRICRIU. I am one of the spirits from the sea.

EMER. What spirit from the sea dares lie upon Cuchulain's bed and take his image?

BRICRIU. I am called Bricriu, Bricriu of the Sidhe. I am maker of discord.

EMER. Come for what purpose?

EITHNE INGUBA. *(terrified)* Ah!

*(**EITHNE INGUBA** runs out.)*

BRICRIU. I show my face and everything he loves must fly away.

EMER. I have not fled your face.

BRICRIU. You are not loved.

EMER. And therefore have no dread to meet your eyes and to demand my husband.

BRICRIU. He is here…

*(He raises his withered arm and points to the **SPIRIT OF CUCHULAIN** across the stage, also behind the scrim.)*

Your lamentations and that woman's lamentations have brought him in a sort of dream, but you can never win him without my help. Come to my left hand and I will touch your eyes and give you sight.

*(He gestures toward her eyes, and she responds as if his withered hand has enabled her to see the **SPIRIT OF CUCHULAIN**, with a mask that resembles that of **CUCHULAIN**'s.)*

EMER. Husband! Husband!

BRICRIU. He seems near, and yet is as much out of reach as though there were a world between. I have made him visible to you. I cannot make you visible to him.

EMER. Cuchulain! Cuchulain!

BRICRIU. Be silent, woman! He can neither see nor hear. But I can give him to you at a price.

(clashing percussive sounds)

Listen to that. Listen to the horses of the sea trampling! Fand, daughter of Manannan, has come. She is reining in her chariot, that is why the horses trample so. She is come to take Cuchulain from you, to take him away forever, but I am her enemy, and I can show you how to thwart her.

EMER. Fand, daughter of Manannan!

BRICRIU. Woman of the Sidhe, yes. While he is still here you can keep him if you pay the price. Once back in Manannan's house, he is lost to you forever.

EMER. There is no price I will not pay.

BRICRIU. You spoke but now of a hope that some day his love may return to you, that some day you may sit by the fire as when first married.

EMER. That is the one hope I have, the one thing that keeps me alive.

BRICRIU. Renounce it, and he shall live again.

EMER. Never, never!

BRICRIU. He'll never sit beside you at the hearth.

EMER. Why should the gods demand such a sacrifice?

BRICRIU. The gods must serve those who living become like the dead.

EMER. I will get him despite the gods, but I will not renounce his love.

*(**GUARDIAN/FAND**, the Woman of the Sidhe, enters behind scrim, with movements and gestures that suggest moving through water.)*

Who is that woman?

BRICRIU. She has hurried from the Country-under-Wave
And dreamed herself into that shape that he
May glitter in her basket; for the Sidhe
Are dexterous fishers and they fish for men
With dreams upon the hook.

EMER.   I know her sort.
They find our men asleep, weary with war,
Lap them in cloudy hair or kiss their lips;
Our men awake in ignorance of it all,
But when we take them in our arms at night
We cannot break their solitude.

(She draws a knife from her girdle.)

BRICRIU.   No knife
Can wound that body of air.

*(**EMER** puts away knife.)*

                    Be silent; listen;
I have not given you eyes and ears for nothing.

SPIRIT OF CUCHULAIN. Who is it stands before me there
Shedding such light from limb and hair
As when the moon, complete at last
With every laboring crescent past,
And lonely with extreme delight,
Flings out upon the fifteenth night?

FAND. Because I long I am not complete.
What pulled your hands about your feet,
Pulled down your head upon your knees,
And hid your face?

SPIRIT OF CUCHULAIN.   Old memories:
A woman in her happy youth
Before her man had broken troth,
Dead men and women. Memories
Have pulled my head upon my knees.

FAND. Could you that have loved many a woman
  That did not reach beyond the human,
  Lacking a day to be complete,
  Love one that, though her heart can beat,
  Lacks it but by an hour or so?

SPIRIT OF CUCHULAIN. I know you now, for long ago
  I met you on a cloudy hill
  Beside old thorn-trees and a well.
  A woman danced and a hawk flew,
  I held out arms and hands; but you,
  That now seem friendly, fled away,
  Half woman and half bird of prey.

FAND. Hold out your arms and hands again;
  You were not so dumbfounded when
  I was that bird of prey, and yet
  I am all woman now.

SPIRIT OF CUCHULAIN.   I am not
  The young and passionate man I was,
  And though that brilliant light surpass
  All crescent forms, my memories
  Weigh down my hands, abash my eyes.

FAND. Then kiss my mouth. Though memory
  Be beauty's bitterest enemy
  I have no dread, for at my kiss
  Memory on the moment vanishes:
  Nothing but beauty can remain.

SPIRIT OF CUCHULAIN. And shall I never know again
  Intricacies of blind remorse?

FAND. When your mouth and my mouth meet
  All my round shall be complete
  Imagining all its circles run.

SPIRIT OF CUCHULAIN.   Your mouth!

  (They are about to kiss, but he turns away.)
  O Emer, Emer!

FAND. So then it is she
Made you impure with memory.

SPIRIT OF CUCHULAIN. O Emer, Emer, there we stand;
Side by side and hand in hand
Tread the threshold of the house
As when we married.

FAND. Being among the dead you love her
That valued every slut above her
While you still lived.

SPIRIT OF CUCHULAIN. O my lost Emer!

FAND. But what could make you fit to wive
With flesh and blood, being born to live
Where no one speaks of broken troth?

SPIRIT OF CUCHULAIN. Your mouth, your mouth!

BRICRIU. Cry out that you renounce his love, cry that you renounce his love forever.

EMER. No, no, never will I give that cry.

BRICRIU. Fool, fool! I am Fand's enemy. I come to tell you how to thwart her and you do nothing. There is yet time. There is still a moment left; cry out, cry out! Renounce his love, and all her power over him comes to an end. Cuchulain's foot is on the step. Cry –

(**EMER** *dances her inner struggle as she works to extract her love for and claim to* **CUCHULAIN**. *The music moves towards dissonance; she collapses; and within a long vibrating note...*)

EMER. I renounce Cuchulain's love forever.

(*Music builds in a resounding crescendo. Blackout behind the scrim, making the figures of* **BRICRIU**, **FAND** *and* **SPIRIT OF CUCULAIN** *vanish at once as* **EMER** *collapses onto stool in front of the scrim.* **EITHNE** *re-enters.*)

EITHNE INGUBA. Cuchulain, Cuchulain! Remember our last meeting? We lay all night among the sand-hills; dawn came; we heard the crying of the birds upon the shore. I come to you, my beloved.

(**CUCHULAIN** *sits up, the grave clothes no longer over his head. He has returned to his body.*)

Look, look! He has come back, he is there in the bed, he has his own rightful form again. It is I who have won him. It is my love that has brought him back to life!

EMER. Cuchulain wakes!

CUCHULAIN. Your arms, your arms! O Eithne Inguba, I have been in some strange place and am afraid.

(**EMER** *watches as* **CUCHULAIN** *embraces* **EITHNE** *and they exit arm and arm.* **THE POET** *watches* **EMER** *and then turns to us.*)

THE POET. A woman's beauty is like a white
Frail bird, like a white sea-bird alone
At daybreak after stormy night
Between two furrows upon the ploughed land:
A sudden storm and it was thrown
Between dark furrows upon the ploughed land.

How many centuries spent
The sedentary soul
In toils of measurement
Beyond eagle or mole,
Beyond hearing or seeing,
Or Archimedes' guess,
To raise into being
That loveliness?

A strange, unserviceable thing,
A fragile, exquisite, pale shell,
That the vast troubled waters bring
To the loud sands before day has broken.
The storm arose and suddenly fell
Amid the dark before day had broken,
What death? What discipline?
What bonds no man could unbind,

Being imagined within
The labyrinth of the mind,
What pursuing or fleeing,
What wounds, what bloody press
Dragged into being
This loveliness?

(As **EMER** *slowly rises and heads in the opposite direction from that of* **CUCHULAIN** *and* **EITHNE***'s exit,* **THE POET** *addresses us about* **EMER***.)*

THE POET. *(cont.)* What makes your heart so beat?
What man is at your side?
When beauty is complete
Your own thought will have died
And danger not be diminished;
Dimmed at three-quarter light,
When moon's round is finished
The stars are out of sight.

*(***EMER** *music ends and a new melody grows out of it as* **CUCHULAIN** *re-enters behind the scrim. He is now wearing an older mask. As he walks, he ages.* **THE POET***'s poem accompanies* **CUCHULAIN***'s walk through time.)*

Who dreamed that beauty passes like a dream?
For these red lips, with all their mournful pride,
Mournful that no new wonder may betide,
Troy passed away in one high funeral gleam,
And Usna's children died.

We and the labouring world are passing by:
Amid men's souls, that waver and give place
Like the pale waters in their wintry race,
Under the passing stars, foam of the sky,
Lives on his lonely face.

Bow down, archangels, in your dim abode:
Before you were, or any hearts to beat,
Weary and kind one lingered by His seat;
He made the world to be a grassy road

Before her wandering feet.

(When the fully aged **CUCHULAIN** *exits, percussive war music changes the mood abruptly.* **MORRIGU***, the goddess of war, appears behind the scrim and whispers "Cuchulain," over and over.* **CUCHULAIN** *re-enters in front of the scrim and responds as if he doesn't know from where his name is called. Then* **AOIFE***, now with white hair, appears from another part of the stage, behind the scrim, also whispering his name.* **EITHNE INGUBA***, now an older woman in her forties, appears from yet another direction and she, too, enters behind the scrim, whispering his name. The whispers build to full voices that haunt and frighten him. The shadowy presence of the three women recalls the three peasant women from Act One. The calling of his name merges with the percussive battle sounds. Blackout behind the scrim but the names and battle sounds continue.* **CUCHULAIN***, a haunted man, is on his knees when* **EITHNE INGUBA** *re-enters in front of the scrim, continuing the calls to "Cuchulain" begun by the three but now as part of this world.)*

EITHNE INGUBA. Cuchulain, Cuchulain! I am Emer's messenger,
  I am your wife's messenger, she has bid me say
  You must not linger here in sloth, for Maeve
  With all those Connacht ruffians at her back
  Burns barns and houses up at Emain Macha:
  Your house at Muirthemne already burns.
  No matter what's the odds, no matter though
  Your death may come of it, ride out and fight.
  The scene is set and you must out and fight.

CUCHULAIN. You have told me nothing. I am already armed,
  I have sent a messenger to gather men,
  And wait for his return. What have you there?

EITHNE INGUBA. I have nothing.

CUCHULAIN.   There is something in your hand.

EITHNE. No.

CUCHULAIN. Have you a letter in your hand?

*(***CUCHULAIN*** takes the letter from her and reads it.)*

EITHNE. I do not know how it got into my hand.
I am straight from Emer. We were in some place.
She spoke. She saw.

CUCHULAIN.   This is a letter from Emer,
It tells a different story. I am not to move
Until tomorrow morning, for, if now,
I must face odds no man can face and live.

EITHNE.   I do not understand.
Who can have put that letter in my hand?

CUCHULAIN. And there is something more to make it certain
I shall not stir till morning; you are sent
To be my bedfellow, but have no fear,
All that is written, but I much prefer
Your own unwritten words. I am for the fight,
I and my handful are set upon the fight;
We have faced great odds before, a straw decided.

(War drums accompany **MORRIGU***'s sudden appearance as the lights blaze behind the scrim. She stands between them. She sees* **MORRIGU** *not by looking back but out over heads of audience.)*

EITHNE. I know that somebody or something is there
Yet nobody that I can see.

CUCHULAIN.   There is nobody.

EITHNE. Who among the gods of the air and upper air
Has a bird's head?

CUCHULAIN.   Morrigu is headed like a crow.

EITHNE. *(dazed)* Morrigu, war goddess, stands between.
Her black wing touched me upon the shoulder, and
All is intelligible.

(Blackout behind the scrim.)

                Maeve put me in a trance.

Though when Cuchulain slept with her as a boy
She seemed as pretty as a bird, she has changed.
She has an eye in the middle of her forehead.

CUCHULAIN. A woman that has an eye in the middle of her
    forehead!
A woman that is headed like a crow!
But she that put those words into your mouth
Had nothing monstrous; you put them there yourself;
You need a younger man, a friendlier man,
But, fearing what my violence might do,
Thought out these words to send me to my death,
And were in such excitement you forgot
The letter in your hand.

EITHNE. What mouth could you believe if not my mouth?

CUCHULAIN. When I went mad at my son's death and drew
My sword against the sea, it was my wife
That brought me back.

EITHNE.   Better women than I
Have served you well, but 'twas to me you turned.

CUCHULAIN. You thought that if you changed I'd kill you
    for it,
When everything sublunary must change,
And if I have not changed that goes to prove
That I am monstrous.

EITHNE.   You're not the man I loved,
That violent man forgave no treachery.
If, thinking what you think, you can forgive,
It is because you are about to die.

CUCHULAIN. Spoken too loudly and too near the door;
Speak low if you would speak about my death,
Or not in that strange voice exulting in it.
Who knows what ears listen behind the door?

EITHNE. Some that would not forgive a traitor, some
That have the passion necessary to life,

Some not about to die. When you are gone
I shall denounce myself to all your cooks,
Scullions, armourers, bed-makers and messengers,
Until they hammer me with a ladle, cut me with a knife,
Impale me upon a spit, put me to death
By what foul way best please their fancy,
So that my shade can stand among the shades
And greet your shade and prove it is no traitor.

CUCHULAIN. Women have spoken so, plotting a man's
    death.

*(**CUCHULAIN** exits.)*

EITHNE. I might have peace that know
    The Morrigu, the woman like a crow,
    Stands to my defence and cannot lie,
    But that Cuchulain is about to die.

*(The stage grows dim as we hear a pipe, drum, and
sounds of combat. **THE POET** attaches a high vertical member to the middle and upstage part of the bed/
platform where **CUCHULAIN** 's body was laid out at the
top of Act Two. **CUCHULAIN** staggers back on, clearly
wounded and works himself up onto the bed/platform
and ties himself to the vertical member as if it were a
pillar of stone. **AOIFE**, an erect white-haired woman,
enters.)*

AOIFE. Am I recognized, Cuchulain?

CUCHULAIN.   You fought with a sword,
    It seemed that we should kill each other, then
    Your body wearied and I took your sword.

AOIFE. But look again, Cuchulain! Look again!

CUCHULAIN. Your hair is white.

AOIFE.   That time was long ago,
    And now it is my time. I have come to kill you.

CUCHULAIN.   I have put my belt
    About this stone and want to fasten it

And die upon my feet, but am too weak.
Fasten this belt.

(She helps him do so.)

                    And now I know your name,
Aoife, the mother of my son. We met
At the Hawk's Well under the withered trees.
I killed him upon Baile's Strand, that is why
Maeve parted ranks that she might let you through.
You have a right to kill me.

AOIFE.   Not a man
Of all that terrified army dare approach,
But I approach.

CUCHULAIN.   Because you have the right.

AOIFE. But I am an old woman now, and that
Your strength may not start up when the time comes,
I wind my veil about this ancient stone
And fasten you to it.

CUCHULAIN.   But do not spoil your veil.
Your veils are beautiful, some with threads of gold.

AOIFE. *(She winds the veil about him.)* I am too old to care for
such things now.

CUCHULAIN. There was no reason so to spoil your veil:
I am weak from loss of blood.

AOIFE.   I was afraid,
But now that I have wound you in the veil,
I am not afraid. But – how did my son fight?

CUCHULAIN. Age makes more skillful but not better men.

AOIFE. I have been told you did not know his name
And wanted, because he had a look of me,
To be his friend.

CUCHULAIN.   I spoke about a look;
But somebody spoke of witchcraft and I said
Witchcraft had made the look, and fought and killed
    him.

Then I went mad, I fought against the sea.

AOIFE. I seemed invulnerable; you took my sword,
You threw me on the ground and left me there.
I searched the mountain for your sleeping-place
And laid my virgin body at your side,
And yet, because you had left me, hated you,
And thought that I would kill you in your sleep,
And yet begot a son that night between
Two black thorn-trees.

CUCHULAIN.   I cannot understand.

AOIFE. Because you're about to die!

(BLIND MAN *enters, tapping his stick.*)

                    Somebody comes,
Some countryman, and when he finds you here,
And none to protect him, will be terrified.
I will keep out of his sight, for I have things
That I must ask questions on before I kill you.

(She exits. BLIND MAN *moves his stick until he finds the
standing stone; he lays stick down, stoops and touches*
CUCHULAIN's *feet and feels his legs.*)

BLIND MAN. Ah! Ah!

CUCHULAIN.   I think you are a blind old man.

BLIND MAN. A blind old beggar-man. What is your name?

CUCHULAIN. Cuchulain.

BLIND MAN.   They say that you are weak with wounds.
I stood between a Fool and the sea at Baile's Strand
When you went mad. What's bound about your hands
So that they cannot move? Some womanish stuff.
I have been fumbling with my stick since dawn
And then heard many voices. I began to beg.
Somebody said that I was in Maeve's tent,
And somebody else, a big man by his voice,
That if I brought Cuchulain's head in a bag
I would be given twelve pennies; I had the bag

> To carry what I get at kitchen doors,
> Somebody told me how to find the place;
> I thought it would have taken till the night,
> But this has been my lucky day.

CUCHULAIN.   Twelve pennies!

BLIND MAN. I would not promise anything until the woman,
> The great Queen Maeve herself, repeated the words.

CUCHULAIN. Twelve pennies! What better reason for killing
> a man?
> You have a knife, but have you sharpened it?

BLIND MAN. I keep it sharp because it cuts my food.

(He lays pouch on ground and begins feeling **CUCHU-LAIN***'s body, his hands mounting upward.)*

CUCHULAIN. I think that you know everything, Blind Man,
> My mother or my nurse said that the blind
> Know everything.

BLIND MAN.   No, but they have good sense.
> How could I have got twelve pennies for your head
> If I had not good sense?

CUCHULAIN.   There floats out there
> The shape that I shall take when I am dead,
> My soul's first shape, a soft feathery shape,
> And is not that a strange shape for the soul
> Of a great fighting-man?

BLIND MAN. *(holds knife to* **CUCHULAIN***'s throat)* Your shoulder
is there,
> This is your neck. Ah! Ah! Are you ready, Cuchulain!

CUCHULAIN. I say it is about to sing.

BLIND MAN.   Ah! Ah!

(Blackout. **THE BLIND MAN,** **CUCHULAIN** *and the vertical unit have vanished from the platform. The lights come back on behind the scrim only.* **MORRIGU** *is there, alone on stage, holding a man's head upon a stake. It is* **CUCHULAIN***'s head, his eyes staring fiercely ahead.*

MORRIGU *places the stake in a hole in the middle of the upstage area behind the scrim and then exits.* **EMER** *enters, also upstage of the scrim, and, accompanied by percussion only, dances her rage against those who have killed* **CUCHULAIN**, *moving in circles around his head, a dance of pain and loss that builds to one of adoration or triumph. She approaches his head, reaches for it but stops and freezes as the percussion sounds climax and cease.* **THE POET**, *who has been watching this scene, focuses first on what he sees behind the scrim, then turns to us.)*

THE POET. Cuchulain stirred,
Stared on the horses of the sea, and heard
The cars of battle and his own named cried;
And fought with the invulnerable tide.

(We begin to hear the sound of the tumultuous sea, which grows louder and louder as we see **CUCHULAIN**'s *fierce eyes staring front,* **EMER**'s *frozen figure with arm stretched in the direction of the head on the stake. Lights fade, followed by a fade in the sound of the sea, until all is black and silent.)*

End of Play

POSTSCRIPT

Sword Against the Sea draws from the six Cuchulain plays that William Butler Yeats wrote over a 35 year period beginning in 1904. The plays, written at different stages of Yeats' career and exploring different themes and styles, were never intended as a cycle, nor were they even written in the chronological order of the hero's life. To perform them in that order without alterations makes for an evening that is not only long and unwieldy, but would also be stylistically bumpy. When the plays are presented individually, the style is consistent, but the evening is too brief, and to show any two of the plays as a double-bill does not convey the full arc of Cuchulain's story. To create an adaptation, then, that is thematically and stylistically whole, structurally sound, and of "proper magnitude," I have had to rework each of the Cuchulain plays internally as well as adopt various textual and staging strategies for transitions between them.

I begin with *At the Hawk's Well* where we see Cuchulain as a young man. The play ends with Cuchulain battling the woman warrior, Aoife, with whom he will father a son. I follow that with a brief wedding scene with lines from *The Green Helmet*, re-contextualizing them into vows that Cuchulain and Emer speak or sing to one another. This sets up Emer's love and devotion vital to the action of Act Two.

Borrowing from an early Yeats poem, I create a scene of Aoife, 20 years later, bidding her son to fight his father. This transitions to *On Baile's Strand*, which introduces Cuchulain at the apogee of his fame as a warrior. In my re-conceiving of *On Baile's Strand*, I resort to radical surgery. I eliminate a major character and a part of the plot I believe distracts from the real issue of the play. By cutting the character of Conchubar and Cuchulain's oath to him, I have sought to tip the weight of responsibility of Cuchulain's filicide toward Cuchulain himself, making his actions more "tragic" in the traditional Aristotelian sense. Removing Conchubar also helps tighten the plot, eliminate extraneous characters, and redirect the focus onto Cuchulain's struggle against a feminized version of fate, which places the play more in harmony with the theme that ties together all of Yeats' Cuchulain plays and poems. A final reason for taking so bold a liberty is to condense a play that is almost twice the size of the other Cuchulain plays and is stylistically the most anomalous. Written much earlier, *On Baile's Strand* predates the influence on Yeats (through Ezra Pound) of the Japanese Nō plays, which, among other features, characteristically includes some form of dance at a key moment in the play's action. In order to bring this play into stylistic conformity with the other Cuchulain plays, then, my version of

On Baile's Strand ends with a Nō-like dance of Cuchulain fighting the waves, an event only described in Yeats' original.

Act Two begins with the middle-aged Cuchulain lying on what seems to be his deathbed from having fought the waves at the end of Act One. The text I use for this section is a combination of *The Only Jealousy of Emer* and Yeats' subsequently rewritten prose version, *Fighting the Waves*. I draw more from the prose version than its more famous verse one to capture the down-to-earth, almost domestic struggle between Cuchulain's wife and mistress. Additionally, to move from prose to the rhymed verse of the scene between Fand and the Spirit of Cuchulain provides a more striking contrast than if that mystical scene were to follow dialogue in just another verse form, as it does in *Jealousy*. It also makes this part of my adaptation more in stylistic alignment with the dominantly prose *On Baile's Strand* that precedes it and sets up an appropriate stylistic contrast with the highly metaphysical verse that distinguishes *The Death of Cuchulain*.

To mark the years between the end of this play and the beginning of the final one, I have borrowed Yeats' poem "The Rose of the World," from his second collection of poems, entitled *The Rose*. This poem, which conveys a feeling of time passing, is spoken as Cuchulain ages as he walks across the stage. This takes us to the final segment of Act Two, corresponding to *The Death of Cuchulain*, when he is an old warrior. Besides making cuts for audiences unfamiliar with Celtic myths and Irish history, my editing is designed to focus on Cuchulain's reckoning with the women of his life and the more body-versus-spirit theme that pervades all of Yeats' Cuchulain works.

I end both Acts One and Two with stanzas from other poems that feature Cuchulain, "To the Rose Upon the Road of Time" and "Cuchulain's Fight with the Sea" as structural bookends for the adaptation as a whole. Not only do these stanzas address similar themes as the Musicians' versified lines in the original Cuchulain plays as Yeats himself wrote them, but they also come at these themes from a similarly oblique angle. But these verse stanzas serve to better lift the Cuchulain story out of a temporal/historical frame into a broader mythic and spiritual one than those built into the ends of the plays by Yeats himself. Moreover, Yeats did not plan to tie these plays together and did not write them as a cycle or in chronological order so one cannot assume that the verses at the end of one Cuchulain play would help transition to the Yeats play about the next stage of Cuchulain's life.

This adaptation is not intended as a substitute for Cuchulain plays as Yeats wrote them; they are theatrical gems just as they are. My interest has only been to adapt Yeats' version of Cuchulain's life journey to a single, stylistically unified work of appropriate length, honed for an audience that may not know or catch Yeats' numerous allusions to Celtic mythology and Irish history. Throughout the adaptation process, I have tried to adhere to the spirit of Yeats' Cuchulain works, the larger intentions behind the individual plays and poems and the threads that unite them. At the same time, I have had to accept that significant alterations needed to be made, even as I weaved the adaptation entirely out of the master's own "embroidered clothes."

- Arthur Feinsod

ABOUT THE PLAYWRIGHT

Arthur Feinsod has been the Artistic Director of Crossroads Repertory Theatre (CRT) in Terre Haute and Professor of Theater at Indiana State University since 2001. Before that, he taught at Trinity College and served as Resident Dramaturg (for Mark Lamos and Bartlett Sher) at Hartford Stage Company. He co-authored with Bill Fennelly an adaptation of *The Legend of Sleepy Hollow*, entitled *The Curse of Sleepy Hollow*, which enjoyed a national tour by the National Theatre of the Deaf in 2000, culminating in presentation at the Bushnell in Hartford. Feinsod's directing credits with Crossroads Rep include: *The School for Wives* (2002); *The Effect of Gamma Rays on Man-in-the-Moon Marigolds* and *The Jewish Wife* (2003); *The Glass Menagerie* and *The Park Bench* (2004); *Plaza Suite* (2005); *A Doll House* (2006); *A Raisin in the Sun* (2007); *The Fantasticks* (2009); *The Sunshine Boys* (2010); *Godspell* (2011); *Return of Neverland* (2012); and *The Servant of Two Masters* (2013). *The Jewish Wife* toured to Mannheim and Heidelberg, Germany as part of the Here and Now Festival in May 2004. *Sword Against the Sea* was part of CRT's 2005 season and was later performed in Sligo, Ireland, co-sponsored by the Yeats Society and under the direction of Sam McCready. Feinsod's play, *Table 17*, staged by Trinidadian director/playwright Tony Hall for the CRT 2007 season, was later presented at the 78th Street Theatre in Manhattan, directed by Dale McFadden. Feinsod is a member of the Dramatists Guild